Schoolies™

My First Day at School

Based on the characters created by
Ellen Crimi-Trent

priddy books

When Spencer woke up,
he had a fluttery thought.

Spencer's tummy flipped and flopped.
He went to see his mum.

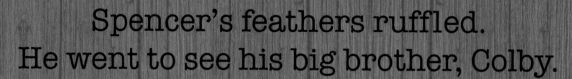

Spencer's feathers ruffled.
He went to see his big brother, Colby.

Spencer's ears twitched.
He put on his roller skates
and felt a little better.

Mr Mouse drove up in the school bus.
Spencer's wings flapped nervously.

Spencer hopped on the bus
and looked around.

Spencer saw friendly faces
smiling at him.

Spencer's ears didn't twitch.
His stomach didn't flip or flop.
His wings still flapped a little, but he smiled.

At school, their teacher Mrs Meow
was waiting for them.

She led the Schoolies inside to
their classroom.

In the classroom, Spencer sat
beside Hayden Hoot.

Straight away, Mrs Meow taught
the Schoolies new things.

Spencer's ears twitched again.
But soon he was counting along with
Hayden, who really loved maths!

Next, Mrs Meow taught them the letters of the alphabet.

During playtime,
the Schoolies went outside.

Spencer was really having fun now!

At lunch time, Spencer's tummy rumbled.

There was lots of good food to eat.
Spencer ate a sandwich and some fruit,
and he drank up all his milk.

Then it was story time. Mrs Meow read
a story about her first day at school.
It was Spencer's favourite part of the day.

All too soon, it was time to go home.
Spencer's feathers drooped.
He would miss all his new friends.

Goodbye!

TOOT!

TOOT!

Mr Mouse drove
the Schoolies hom

Back at home, Spencer told his mum every new thing that had happened at school.

Lucky Spencer, you get to go back again tomorrow!

Really?

Spencer's ears twitched, his feathers flapped and he jumped for joy!